LITTLE MONSTER AT SCHOOL

by Mercer Mayer

to Sonora

MERRIGOLD PRESS • NEW YORK

Library of Congress Catalog Card Number: 77-90845 ISBN: 0-307-03935-8 MCMXCI

Early in the morning, Mom wakes me and says, “Get up, Little Monster, it’s time for school.”

HERO
WAKE UP EARLY. SCHOOL TOMORROW
MY ROOM

I put on my overalls and go downstairs to breakfast. Pop says, "What will you have this morning,

MILK

or with ?"

ONSTER NEWS

crayons
lunchbox
pencils
notebook
apple for the teacher

After breakfast, I brush my teeth and get ready to go. I have lots of school stuff to carry with me.

Mom walks me to school.
Some of my friends come on a bus.

SCHOOL

The first thing we do is sing a morning song and then we practice our letters. Yally makes some of his letters backwards and then he gets mad. But I help him.

Counting comes next. We count from one to twenty. Little Laff is the best counter in the class and that makes Yally mad, too. Yally wants to be the best counter in the class.

Don't be mad. You can count better than me.

We have pets to take care of. I have a Zipperump-a-zoo. Little Laff has a gerbil. Grendella has a snake. Yally won't take care of a pet. He says they're icky.

We grow plants. Everyone is growing something different. I'm growing some beans in a box. Yally's plant won't grow. He says the plant is mad at him.

Yally, you have to water your plant or it won't grow.
BEANS

We tell what we did over the weekend.
Yally makes up the most fantastic stories.

On nice days, lunch time is outside. I have a sandwich and a tango, but Yally always brings lots of candy.

Yally, you shouldn't eat somuch candy.
DO NOT LITTER

At recess, we all go to the playground.
Yally won't play with anyone. He says games are stupid.

Hey, Yally, do you want to play ball?

STORY TIME
LITTLE MONSTER
AND THE
THREE PEOPLE

After recess, Mr. Grithix reads us the story of Little Monster and the Three People. Everyone sits on a mat and listens except Yally, who pouts. He wants to hear a story about horrible people from outer space.

Oh, he doesn't like anything.
Don't pout, Yally, we'll read a story You'll like next time.
cheer up!
ANOTHER STORY

Mr. Grithix gets out a map and shows us where our town is. We see how the monsters dress in different countries, and look at flags from different monster lands.

We have science class and learn about leaves and rocks and bugs.

Then we get to make things. I make a paper airplane, Little Laff makes a block building, and Grendella makes a puppet.

Yally draws the best pictures in the whole class.

Yally draws a great picture and everyone is amazed, especially Yally. Grendella says to Yally, "Yally, you're the best drawer in school." And Yally smiles.

I'll trade you my paper airplane for your picture.
Do you really want my picture?
wow! You're good, Yally.

Then we have singing.
Ms. Verakisser plays the piano.
Yally and I share a songbook,
and Yally even sings.

School is over. I walk home with my older sister and my new friend Yally.

I put Yally's great drawing on my refrigerator, right next to my great drawings.

THE END
Me
MOM
POP
FOR LITTLE MONSTER
YOUR FRIEND YALLY